Nightm Mystery Mansion

Phil Roxbee Cox

Illustrated by Sue Hellard

Designed by Lindy Dark

Edited by
Michelle Bates

Series Editor: Gaby Waters

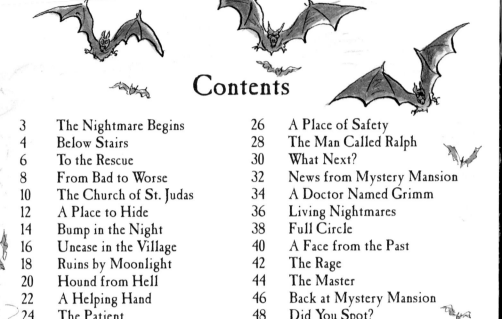

Contents

Reader Beware . . .

This is a chilling ghost story – but there's more to it than meets the eye. The mystery will unravel as the story unfolds, but if you keep your eyes open you may be able to stay one step ahead of the action.

Vital information might be lurking anywhere. On almost every double page there are things that could help you. The pictures are important, so look at them carefully. But don't be fooled. There may be some false clues . . .

Page 48 will give you some hints of what to look out for. You can refer to this page as you go along or look at it at the end to see if you missed anything.

The Nightmare Begins

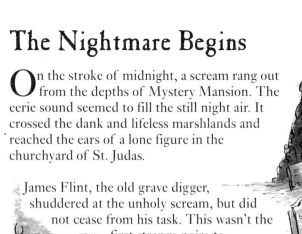

On the stroke of midnight, a scream rang out from the depths of Mystery Mansion. The eerie sound seemed to fill the still night air. It crossed the dank and lifeless marshlands and reached the ears of a lone figure in the churchyard of St. Judas.

James Flint, the old grave digger, shuddered at the unholy scream, but did not cease from his task. This wasn't the first strange noise to come from Mystery Mansion, and he didn't suppose it would be the last. He mopped his sweating brow with a large, ragged handkerchief, then tossed another spadeful of soil over his shoulder. There were still two more graves to be dug that night . . .

A noise, much closer this time, caused Flint to look up with a start. He thought he saw two eyes staring at him from the silhouette of a yew tree.

"Who's there?" he demanded. He tried to sound confident, but the scream had unsettled him and his voice squeaked with fear.

Then he saw the animal, staring down at him in the space he had dug for a coffin. At first, the grave digger thought that it was an enormous hound. Then he realized that it was a wolf. And not just any wolf. It was the wolf that had stalked his dreams for over sixty years.

A second scream filled the air. This time, it came from the churchyard. This time, it was the very human scream of James Flint himself.

Below Stairs

Life was hard for the servants at Mystery Mansion. So hard, that they called it *Misery* Mansion, but not in front of Mr. Paulfrey. Mr. Paulfrey was the head butler and the most important servant in the house.

There were twenty-eight servants at Mystery Mansion and, according to Mr. Paulfrey, Harry Grubb was the least important of them all. Harry was the boot boy and, like all the other servants, lived in fear of Mr. Paulfrey.

You're the lowest of the low, Grubb.

Harry's job of cleaning all the boots and shoes not only kept him tired and dirty, but also kept him 'below stairs'. This meant that he wasn't allowed into the rooms occupied by Lord Rakenhell, the master of Mystery Mansion, or those of his family.

There was only one person that the servants feared more than Mr. Paulfrey, and that was his Lordship. Though few servants had ever met Lord Rakenhell face-to-face, all had heard his cries of rage.

In fact, there were only two people Harry Grubb liked in the whole house. One was Anna, a dusting duty maid, and the other was Miss Charlotte, Lord Rakenhell's only daughter. In the case of Miss Charlotte, he only liked her from a distance. He had never actually *spoken* to her.

All that was to change one December morning. Harry had been instructed by the cook to take a message to Tom Liddle, the gamekeeper, who lived in a cottage on the other side of the estate. It was bitterly cold, so Harry decided to run there to keep warm. The cold air stung his reddened cheeks. Thick frost crunched beneath his feet, and rows of icicles hung from many of the trees he dashed past.

As he came to the edge of a rose garden, he saw smoke from a bonfire coiling up into the crisp morning air like a charmed snake leaving its basket. He stopped to warm himself in front of the crackling flames and thought of the fireplace in the attic room of Mystery Mansion that he shared with three other boys. They were only given one piece of coal to burn each night. He shuddered. How he *hated* Mystery Mansion.

Harry's thoughts were interrupted by a voice barking: "It's Grubb, isn't it?" Harry looked up to see Mr. Colly, the head gardener, staring at him.

"Yes, Mr. Colly," he replied.

"What are you doing here? Shouldn't you be working back at the house?" the gardener asked. Harry told him about the message he had to deliver to Tom Liddle, the gamekeeper.

"Then you can do something for me too," said Mr. Colly. "Instead of crossing the river at Ford's Bridge to reach Liddle's cottage, cross it farther down where the old tree has fallen across it. Do you know where I mean?" Harry nodded, watching the gardener's words turn to steam as they left his mouth and came into contact with the cold air.

"Good. Well, when you've crossed the river, you'll see an old hollow tree just off to your right. I want you to put a parcel in the trunk of the tree." Colly rummaged around in a wheelbarrow and produced a parcel wrapped in brown paper.

Tell no one. Is that understood? No one.

"Yes, Mr. Colly," said Harry. He tucked the parcel under his arm and set off at a sprint. The new route would take him longer, and he didn't want Cook complaining that he'd deliberately taken his time to get out of doing other work.

He hurried through the fields until, up ahead, he could see the tree which had fallen across the river the summer-before-last. Then he heard a voice. It was coming from the river. It was a girl's voice crying out for help.

5

To the Rescue

Harry dashed over to the riverbank and looked over the edge. Instead of flowing water, he was faced by a sheet of ice. The river had frozen over!

The ice looked thick, but obviously not thick enough to support the weight of a child for, to his left, he could see that Charlotte Rakenhell had fallen through the ice and was now up to her shoulders in freezing water.

"Help me! Please help me!" she wailed. Harry rushed over to the fallen tree and broke off one of the branches. Dragging it across the ground, he swung one end over the river bank to within the girl's reach.

"Grab the end of this, Miss Charlotte," he shouted. "I'll pull you out." Lord Rakenhell's frightened daughter clutched her end of the branch, and Harry pulled with all his might. He heard her yelp with pain as she rubbed against the jagged ice and was pulled up the bank to safety.

Charlotte lay on the ground gasping for breath and shivering. On her feet were a pair of ice skates. "You must get out of your wet clothes before you catch your death of cold, Miss Charlotte," said Harry.

Charlotte's eyes widened. "What would I change into?" she asked, her teeth chattering like clattering knitting needles.

"At least take off your coat and wear this," Harry urged. Slipping off his old jacket, he held it out to her. Without a word, she did as he suggested.

Harry knew he must get her back to the house to dry out and warm up. "Take off your skates, Miss," he said, hurrying over to where she'd left her winter boots. He brought them to Charlotte and helped her put them on.

They ran across the fields toward Mystery Mansion. Charlotte was shivering so much now that Harry changed his plan and led her to Mr. Colly's bonfire.

"Warm yourself as best you can, miss," he said. "I'll see if I can find you some more dry clothes." Harry went into the potting shed and found a pair of gardening gloves, a smock and a battered hat. Fortunately, Mr. Colly was nowhere to be seen. Charlotte went into the shed and came out dressed in the dry clothes. Harry couldn't help smiling when he saw her. She looked like a scarecrow.

"What are you laughing at – ?" she began. Then, as the warmth started to return to her bones, she smiled. "I suppose I must look rather silly. What's your name? I've seen you up at the house." Harry told her. "Well, thank you for saving me, Harry, but it must be our secret. My father would be very angry if he knew that I'd been skating on my own. He'd be even more angry if he heard I'd had an accident. You must promise to tell no one," she ordered.

"I promise, miss," said Harry. "But, if you'll forgive me asking, how will you explain your clothes?"

"If anyone asks, I shall say that I have been dressing up. I am a Rakenhell, so no one will dare argue with me. Please take my wet clothes to the laundry room for me," she said, handing them to him.

As Harry took the bundle from her, his heart sank. It reminded him of the package Mr. Colly had given him. He must have dropped it by the river bank when he had rescued Miss Charlotte! And he still hadn't delivered Cook's message to the gamekeeper. He would be in big trouble.

From Bad to Worse

Harry hunted high and low for the package, but without success. In the end, he gave up looking and delivered Cook's message to the gamekeeper. He then returned to Mystery Mansion. Slipping into the laundry room, he hid Miss Charlotte's wet things in among some other clothes.

As he tiptoed into the corridor, he walked bang into Mr. Paulfrey. "What have you been doing?" the butler snarled.

"I've just been delivering a message to Tom Liddle for Cook, Mr. P-P-Paulfrey," Harry stammered.

"You should have been back over an hour ago, boy," said the butler. "I think you've been hiding in the nice warm laundry room instead of working. You shall have to be punished. Are you afraid of good, honest hard work and a little cold weather?"

"N-No, sir," said Harry, thinking that, if life were fair, he would have been hailed a hero for saving Miss Charlotte's life. Instead, he was facing punishment.

Punishments for servants at Mystery Mansion had to be carefully planned. There was no point in locking someone in his or her room because it would probably be more fun than working! Sometimes, servants who had angered Mr. Paulfrey went without food. Once a maid had been made to eat a lump of coal for stealing a bread roll.

Harry Grubb's punishment was very simple. He had to clean all the boots and shoes that he would have had to clean anyway – only he had to do it outside in the freezing cold. The scullery maids were under strict instructions to make sure that he didn't come inside until the very last shoe was polished. They all felt sorry for Harry – especially Anna – but, at the same time, none of them dared disobey Mr. Paulfrey.

After a while, Harry began shivering as much as Charlotte had been when he had rescued her. His body was covered in goose bumps, and his fingers were stiff with cold. He couldn't hold the shoebrush properly and he felt like crying.

8

"Harry!" a voice called out. The boot boy looked around the courtyard, but couldn't see anyone. "Harry!" the voice called again. This time he spotted Charlotte at a window. She was wearing a thick purple dress and looked none the worse for her icy swim. "What's going on?"

When Harry had finished explaining, Charlotte looked outraged. "Well, I am ordering you to go back inside, and tell Cook to give you some warm soup," she said. "Is that clear?"

"Y-Y-Yes, miss," said Harry. Nothing like this had ever happened at Mystery Mansion before.

At first, Cook couldn't believe her ears when Harry shuffled into the kitchen and explained that he'd been ordered to ask for soup. But soon she realized that he wouldn't dare make up such a story, and poured him a steaming bowlful.

When the news reached Mr. Paulfrey, he was furious and he stormed into the

kitchen. "I expect you're feeling very pleased with yourself, Grubb," he said. "But remember this – Miss Rakenhell took pity on you this afternoon, but has probably forgotten you already. I, on the other hand, will not forget . . . and *I* see you every day. Back to work!"

In the warmth of the boot room, Harry set about his tasks when a figure appeared in the doorway. It was Mr. Colly. "You didn't deliver my package!" he whispered. "What have you done with it?" Harry groaned. How he hated Mystery Mansion.

The Church of St. Judas

The following day, there were four burials in the churchyard of St. Judas. Three of these were for men who had strayed from one of the paths through the misty marshland and had sunk in boggy ground.

The marshland around Mystery Mansion seemed to be governed by its own rules of nature. Paths that were safe one week became dangerous the next. Few local people dared to cross the marsh, with its strange mists and eerie yellow night-time glow.

The fourth funeral was for James Flint, the grave digger. He had rushed home in the middle of the night, screaming something about 'wolves', and died, exhausted, in his bed. This hadn't surprised many villagers. Most of them had thought that old Jimmy Flint had been strange all his life.

As the last of the mourners left the last of the funerals, Magnus Duggan, the clock winder, went inside the church of St. Judas. These last few nights he'd been sleeping badly. Noises kept on waking him . . . noises that came from the heart of Mystery Mansion.

When Duggan wasn't being kept awake at night, he was having nightmares – usually the *same* nightmare, over and over again. As he put away the hymn books, he thought he heard a scuffling noise coming from somewhere in the bell tower.

10

A few weeks before, he had found the local vagabond, Struan Maggot, fast asleep at the back of the church. A storm had been raging outside, and it was a warm, dry place to be. The clock winder couldn't really blame Struan for being there. However, if the vagabond was sleeping in the church again, Duggan would have to have stern words with him.

The clock winder strode across the cold stone floor and threw open the door. "Who's there?" he called. There was no reply. Although it was still daylight outside, the spiral staircase inside the bell tower was dark and forbidding. There were no lights inside the tower.

Magnus Duggan began walking slowly up the stairs. "Is there anybody there?" he asked. He listened and, above the pounding of his own heart, he heard a definite scuffling up ahead.

H-Hello?

This was ridiculous. He had been clock winder at St. Judas for many years, and had never felt in the slightest bit scared before. It was those awful nightmares, that were making him feel so uneasy now . . .

Suddenly, a moving shadowy mass seemed to appear from nowhere, and surround him. Magnus Duggan screamed. He saw bats. Hundreds of them. He screamed again and fell back down the stairs . . . just as he had in his nightmares.

A Place to Hide

Three weeks passed, the weather worsened and Harry the boot boy didn't hear any more from Mr. Colly about the undelivered package. Perhaps Mr. Colly had searched along the riverbank and found it himself? Harry didn't think it very likely. But one thing seemed clear. Mr. Colly didn't want anyone to know about the errand.

That made two secrets he had to keep. He was bursting to tell Anna, the maid, about saving Miss Charlotte's life. But he had kept his promise to Lord Rakenhell's daughter, and said nothing.

Christmas drew nearer. Not that Christmas was a festive time for the servants at Mystery Mansion. At this time of year, they didn't call it *Misery* Mansion but *Miserly* Mansion. No one was given any time off. They had no fun and no parties. Mr. Paulfrey and a reluctant Mrs. Weatherspoon, the housekeeper, were the only ones to have a special Christmas meal.

Every year, Mr. Paulfrey gave instructions that any leftovers from the enormous feast, which Lord Rakenhell enjoyed with his family, should be fed to the dogs. Not so much as a mingy morsel should pass the other servants' lips.

It was the week before Christmas when Charlotte Rakenhell and Harry Grubb spoke to each other again. Charlotte was having a party with the children of other rich landowners in the district. There were well-fed children in expensive clothes running all over Mystery Mansion.

Not all of the children who had been invited had come, however. Some parents had heard stories of the strange noises coming from the house, and didn't want them visiting it.

You're not going there, Arabella. It's a bad place.

Charlotte wanted to play a kind of hide-and-seek where everyone ends up hiding in the same place. She wanted to be the first person to hide and needed a really good hiding place. Who better to ask than a servant, who used parts of the house she had never been in? Everyone would be hunting for her for hours. She went to the boot room and found Harry hard at work as always.

"Don't you get bored doing that all day?" she asked.

Harry looked up in surprise. "No, Miss Charlotte," he said. "I mean, it's the only thing I know how to do. Who knows, one day I might be a butler like Mr. Paulfrey."

"A butler, perhaps, Harry, but not like Paulfrey I hope. He's such a horrid man. I don't know why Papa puts up with him," Charlotte sighed. Then she told him about needing a good hiding place.

Harry knew such a place. There was a big storage cupboard that wasn't used any more, down at the end of the corridor joining the servants' quarters to the main part of the house. The door to the cupboard was hidden behind an old tapestry. Unless you knew it was there, it would take ages to find it.

"Come on, Miss Charlotte. I'll show you," he said. He led her down the corridor and pulled back the tapestry. "Here," he said, triumphantly.

"You expect me and all my friends to be able to hide behind one mangy old tapestry?" she laughed. "We're not that thin."

"No. There's a storage cupboard here . . ." he began, turning to point out the hidden door. Only there was no door to be seen, just a blank wall. The door had disappeared.

13

Bump in the Night

That night, Harry's dreams were filled with terrible images of the evil Mr. Paulfrey. He woke with a start to find Anna shaking his shoulder. She wasn't allowed in this part of the house. They would both be in *big* trouble if she had been seen. Without waking the other boys in the room, they tiptoed out into the passageway.

"What is it?" he whispered.

"There are some strange new noises downstairs," Anna whispered back. "Different from the usual moaning and wailing."

All that Harry could hear was snoring coming from the other servants' bedrooms. "I don't hear anything," he said.

"I didn't say you could hear them from up here," she said. "I went downstairs to look for that silver locket my mother gave me. I lost it this afternoon and wanted to see if I could find it before we started work in the morning. Then I heard the noises. They're coming from under the floor. Come on."

Before Harry could stop her, Anna was creeping down the servants' stairs. Neither Mr. Paulfrey nor Mrs. Weatherspoon would take kindly to them wandering around at night. It was strictly against the rules.

When they reached the kitchen, Harry wanted to turn back. The servants often heard strange cries at night, but Mr. Paulfrey's instructions were clear. No one was even to mention them.

14

They entered the kitchen just as a loud groaning noise came from beneath the floor. It sounded like a wounded animal. Harry wished that he was back in his hard bed in the cold attic room.

"It's not like any of the other weird noises I've heard lately," whispered Anna. "It sounds almost human."

Harry took a candle from a shelf, lighting it from the one Anna was holding. A cockroach appeared from under a table and scurried over his bare feet. He shuddered. Harry held out his candle and looked at the floor to see if there were any other insects patrolling the huge flagstones under cover of darkness. His eyes were caught by the movement of one of the flagstones to the right of him. Grabbing Anna, he pulled her around to the other side of the kitchen table. She blew out both of the candles.

Moments later, a new light shone out. A man was coming out from under the flagstone, lantern in hand. It must be a secret trap door. The stranger held the lantern high as a second person emerged from the trap door. It was none other than Mrs. Weatherspoon.

"Oh, I'll make him talk, don't you worry," the man told her.

A groan sounded from beneath the floor once more . . . a very human groan. The hairs on the back of Harry's neck stood up. He shuddered.

He'll talk. Give me time.

Unease in the Village

That same night, across the marshes at *The Bogside Inn*, the villager Thora Mulch was doing what she did best. Gossiping. If there was anything worth knowing in the village, she was the first to find it out. It was she who pointed out that local folk were having terrible nightmares and that some of their bad dreams were coming true.

"Old Jimmy Flint was haunted by the dreams of a wolf, but how many of you know that he had scratch marks on his face when he died?" she asked a group of men. The landlord of *The Bogside Inn* put the tankard he was polishing on the counter.

"The scratches could have been made by thorns, Thora. The churchyard at St. Judas is overgrown in parts," he reasoned. "And, from what I hear, real, live wolves are harmless beasts anyhow."

"Thorns?" scoffed Thora Mulch. "Harmless? They say that the scratches were like deep, deep, claw marks. And what about poor Mr. Duggan? He's been clock winder for I don't know how long. He must have been up and down those steps in the bell tower a thousand times. Only now he starts having nightmares about bats and suddenly he's attacked by a whole swarm of them. He's lucky he didn't break his neck, falling down them stairs."

16

"How is he now?" asked a man who was leaning on the bar, a tankard of foaming ale in his hand.

"Disappeared, that's how he is," said Thora Mulch. "The last anyone saw of him, he was in bed with a sore back and a bandage on his head. Now he's disappeared into thin air. This isn't the first disappearance. Mark my words, it has something to do with the big house. It ain't called *Mystery* Mansion for nothing."

The landlord laughed. "You're not talking to a bunch of outsiders now, Thora," he said. "We all know how Mystery Mansion got its name."

The village gossip snorted indignantly. "So you believe it was called *Misty* Mansion when it was built, do you?" she demanded.

"Of course I do," said the landlord. "It makes perfect sense to call the place Misty Mansion. It's always surrounded by mist from the marshlands. That filthy marsh gas is everywhere. Its name just changed over the years. It's as simple as that."

"The Rakenhells must have been crazy to build their home here," said Thora, eager to steer the conversation back to the strange happenings. "*Misty* or *Mystery*, there's something mighty odd happening in these parts."

Across the eerie, glowing marshland, Mystery Mansion rose out of the mist. Here, Harry and Anna's nightmares had only just begun.

There's evil in that house across the marshes.

Ruins by Moonlight

Back at the mansion, Harry and Anna remained crouched in the darkness long after Mrs. Weatherspoon and the stranger had shut the trap door and left the kitchen.

Harry's brain was reeling – trying to make sense of the extraordinary events they had just witnessed. What had the stranger said? *I'll make him talk.* Who talk? Who else was down there . . . and why wouldn't he talk? Harry had visions of someone being held prisoner in a secret cellar beneath the kitchen. Someone who was being tortured to tell some important secret, but who refused to speak . . . He thought back to the groans coming from beneath the floor.

Mrs. Weatherspoon was obviously a part of whatever was happening, but what about Mr. Paulfrey? This sort of thing couldn't be going on at Mystery Mansion without him knowing about it. In fact, whatever was taking place in the cellar, Harry was willing to bet that the butler was something to do with it. He was such a cruel and evil man. Who could he and Anna turn to? They wouldn't dare speak to Lord Rakenhell, whose furious face glared down on them from so many portraits throughout the house.

The following night, Harry and Anna arranged to hide in the kitchen and watch the trap door. Hours passed, and nothing happened. There were no strange noises or visitors. Anna was almost dozing off, when she spotted a light through the kitchen window. Someone was moving inside the ruins of the chapel on the far end of the sloping lawn. She beckoned Harry over and they looked out into the night.

Three human figures were moving about between the crumbling walls and broken pillars. Each one of them held a lantern, the light from which glinted against the chapel's one remaining stained glass window.

"What shall we do now?" asked Anna.

"Go to the ruined chapel and investigate, of course," whispered Harry.

The chapel had been built at the same time as the house, but whereas Mystery Mansion had been built on rock, the chapel had been built on land that wasn't as firm as the builders had imagined. Within a hundred years, it had started to collapse.

The villagers had said that it was a sign from God. The then Lord Rakenhell had said it was the sign of a bad builder. The chapel had been left as a ruin and never repaired.

Harry and Anna stole across the moonlit lawn, carefully keeping to the shadows. Crouching behind the base of an enormous pillar, they spied on the figures before them. One was the man who had come out of the trap door the night before. The second was Mr. Paulfrey – so Harry had been right. But it was the sight of the third figure that really caused Harry to draw a sharp breath.

Hissing instructions through gritted teeth was someone both Harry and Anna had only ever seen in paintings. It was Lord Rakenhell himself. "Dig man! Dig!" he ordered, lighting an area of grass with his lantern. Mr. Paulfrey thrust the tip of his shovel into the marshy ground.

Harry had the feeling that he and Anna were uninvited guests at a burial.

Hound from Hell

Anna and Harry crouched as still as statues, watching the digging with gruesome fascination. What dark deed was Lord Rakenhell involved in? Whatever it was, no one was going to take a boot boy's word against the Lord of Mystery Mansion.

Harry watched in amazement as Mr. Paulfrey dug deep into the soil. What was happening? Neither he nor Anna had ever seen the butler getting his hands dirty before. He shuddered as the spade glinted in the moonlight.

Harry's thoughts were interrupted by a growl. It was a menacing growl that the boot boy and the dusting duty maid knew only too well – the growl of Lazarus, Lord Rakenhell's pet hound. This was a dog so big and so mean that no one, except Lord Rakenhell and Mr. Paulfrey, would go near him.

Before they knew it, Lazarus was launching his huge hairy body at them. Harry and Anna didn't stop to think. They didn't have time to worry about being seen. They fled.

"After them!" yelled Lord Rakenhell. His voice rang out like the crack of a whip in the darkness.

Harry and Anna ran for their lives. Harry could actually feel the warmth of Lazarus's breath at his ankles. The beast's snarling, slavering jaws only narrowly missed his flesh.

Breathless, and with pains in his side, Harry clambered over a low wall and kept on running. Anna was ahead of him now but, far more seriously, the hound was still behind him. Mist swirled out of nowhere, blotting out the moon. The darkness covered them like a shroud. "Where are you?" Anna cried out.

"Don't worry about me!" he shouted. "Just keep running." There was another snarl from Lazarus who was so close to Harry that Harry almost screamed in terror. This was a living nightmare.

In that instant, Harry felt the ground give way beneath his feet. They were on marshland . . . and he was sinking. Harry was about to shout a warning to Anna when Lazarus appeared out of the mist and gripped his arm between his snarling jaws. He didn't know which would be worse – drowning or being ripped to shreds . . .

A Helping Hand

Just as Harry thought his end had come, a horrid figure appeared, his head wrapped in bandages. Grabbing the dog by the collar, the awful stranger muttered a stern command. The dog released his vice-like grip on Harry's arm then, tail between his legs, trotted off into the night.

"Do exactly as I say and you shall be safe," said the stranger. Despite his terrifying appearance, Harry felt much calmer now the man was here. "You mustn't struggle. The more you wriggle, the quicker the ground will swallow you up."

Harry stayed absolutely still and grasped the man's hands. He found himself being pulled from the swamp like a cork being pulled from the neck of a bottle. Moments later, he found himself standing on the safety of solid ground.

"Thank you," gasped Harry.

The stranger thrust a filthy rag into his hand. "Hold this over your face," he ordered. "It's important not to breath in too much of this foul-smelling mist." A sudden surge of panic welled up inside Harry. He had been so pleased to be rescued that he'd forgotten Anna.

"Anna," he cried. "What about Anna?" The bandaged man grabbed Harry's wrist.

"Keep your voice down," he urged. "Do you want Lord Rakenhell to hear you? Don't go running off again, it's too dangerous. I know the safe paths through here, even by night, but you could perish without me to lead you." Harry frantically explained that he hadn't been alone. "I'll be back for her," began the man. Just then, a familiar voice wafted through the mist. It was the voice of Lord Rakenhell.

"Whoever they are, they must have stumbled into the marsh, poor devils," he said. "There's no hope for them now."

"Fools!" said Mr. Paulfrey. "Serves them right for prying into other people's affairs."

"Rather a harsh lesson," came the third voice, belonging to the man Harry had seen in the kitchen. The party turned and headed back to the chapel, where their task still awaited them. Harry shuddered and turned to face his rescuer.

"You must come with me," said the stranger with the bandaged face. "You must tread where I tread. Sidestep where I sidestep. One false move and you could end up sinking faster than I can pull you out. Ready?" Harry nodded. "Good," said the man. "And remember. Keep the cloth over your face."

Slowly, they began their treacherous journey across the marshland. Harry was worried about Anna, but tried hard to concentrate. Who was his strange rescuer? Did he really live out here in the wilds of the marsh? And what horrors lurked beneath those brown-stained bandages? The man had certainly saved his life, but to what end? Where were they going? Was he being led to a fate worse than being sucked into the depths of the earth? . . .

Then the wailing began. It seemed to be coming from everywhere. Harry peered through the mist and screamed in terror. He saw the boggy ground fill with skeletons, arms outstretched, moaning to be saved.

The Patient

Meanwhile, not far away, Magnus Duggan woke up with a groan. An aching in his head pounded like a blacksmith's hammer on an anvil. He tried to focus, but everything was a blur. A face came into view, but he didn't recognize the features.

"Hello, Mr. Duggan," said a woman. There was kindness in her voice. A cold sponge was wiped across his forehead. It felt refreshingly good. "How are you feeling today?"

Duggan struggled to say that he was feeling a little better, but couldn't form the words. They came out as meaningless grunts. The kind woman patted his arm. "Don't worry," she reassured him. "The words will come with time. You're in good hands here."

The clock winder wondered where *'here'* was. He could remember falling down the stairs after seeing all those bats . . . the bats from his terrible nightmares. He could remember being taken back to his little cottage on the edge of the marsh, but the rest was a blank. The next thing he could recall was drifting in and out of sleep and waking up wherever he was now.

"W-W-Wuramee?" he said, after great effort. The blurred image of the woman's face came closer as she leaned over him to try to catch what he was saying.

"Wuramee?" he repeated.

24

"*Worry me?* Is that what you're trying to say? I'm sorry," said the woman. "I can't understand. The doctor will be here again soon."

Inside his head, Magnus Duggan was trying to ask *'Where am I?'* but it just wouldn't come out right. He felt so frustrated. The pounding in his head grew worse.

A square of light was carved out of the darkness above him. He could hear the rumble of voices followed by footsteps. The blurred image of the kind woman was replaced by that of a man.

"How is he?" he asked, lifting Duggan's right arm and taking his pulse.

"Much better. He's even trying to speak now, doctor," said the woman.

So this man is a doctor, thought Duggan. But this isn't a hospital. If only I could think straight.

Another person loomed into view. There was no mistaking who this was. "Are you still having nightmares, Mr. Duggan?" asked Lord Rakenhell with a smile.

A Place of Safety

When Harry opened his eyes, it was daytime and he was no longer trekking through the marsh. In fact, the first thing he saw was Anna, and she was very much alive and well. He was so pleased to see her.

"It's about time you woke up," she grinned. "You've been asleep for ages." Harry looked around the strange room he was in. It was small, but bright and warm.

"Tell me it was all a dream," he said. "Mr. Paulfrey digging in the chapel at the dead of night . . . Lazurus chasing us . . . those skeletons all coming to life."

"You must have imagined the skeletons," Anna smiled. "But I'm afraid the rest certainly happened." She shuddered, remembering it all.

"You were lucky you didn't get sucked into the marsh," said Harry.

"I lost you in the mist . . . I couldn't see or hear you," Anna recalled. "Then something incredible happened. I thought I saw my dead mother. Her ghost led me along the only safe path . . . she saved me. Then Ralph found me and brought me here."

"Who's Ralph?" asked Harry.

26

"I am," said a tall and rather handsome man walking into the room. "We've already met, but I had my head wrapped in bandages. Remember?"

Harry remembered all right. This was the man who had saved him from the jaws of Lazarus and the damp grave of the marshland. "Thank you for saving my life, sir," he said.

"Forget the *sir*," smiled Ralph with a flash of brilliant white teeth. "You're not at Mystery Mansion now."

At the mention of Mystery Mansion, Harry's heart sank. Both he and Anna would have been reported missing. It wouldn't have taken Mr. Paulfrey long to put two and two together. The butler would soon realize that they were the ones who had been spying on the night-time activities by the chapel – that they were the ones who had been chased by Lazarus.

"At least they won't be searching for you two," said Ralph. He took a log from a basket and started a small fire in the grate. "Lord Rakenhell seemed to think you were both drowned in the marsh."

"But our duties – " began Anna.

"Do you mean to tell me you *want* to go back to work there?" asked Ralph in disbelief.

"We've nowhere else to go, sir," said Harry. He couldn't help calling his rescuer 'sir' because he was trained to address gentlemen in that manner. And Ralph was obviously a gentleman.

"I'm sorry," he said. "Of course not. It was a stupid thing to say."

There was something instantly likeable about Ralph, but what was he doing wandering around the marshes, his head wrapped in bandages? And how had he managed to control Lazarus? *Who* exactly was this man? And could he be trusted?

The Man Called Ralph

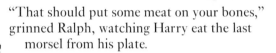

Ralph cooked Harry and Anna the biggest and best breakfast they'd ever eaten before. At Mystery Mansion, breakfast was usually a slice of bread with a smear of grease instead of butter. Ralph fried them bacon, sausages, eggs, fried bread . . . the menu seemed endless. It wasn't only the best breakfast Harry had ever had, it was the best *meal* he'd ever had in his whole life.

"That should put some meat on your bones," grinned Ralph, watching Harry eat the last morsel from his plate.

The mention of bones reminded Harry of the skeletons he had seen in the night. He shivered. They were as real to him as Anna and Ralph were now.

"Can I ask you a few questions Ralph?" he asked.

"Go ahead," said Ralph. "If I were in your shoes, there would be plenty of questions I'd be itching to ask."

Harry wasn't sure where to begin. "Why did you have bandages wrapped around your head when you rescued me last night?" he started.

His rescuer grinned. "Three reasons. One, to frighten people who might see me skulking about. Two, so that nobody will recognize me. And three, so that I don't breathe in all that horrible marsh gas."

"What's marsh gas?" asked Anna.

"It's the mist that you see hovering above the marshes," said Ralph. "Sometimes it even casts an eerie glow in the dark. It's a gas made by all the different chemicals in the rotting vegetation in the mud and water. It can be dangerous if you breathe in too much. That's why I made you both hold cloths over your faces."

28

"But why should you want to frighten people?" asked Harry. "You've been so kind to us." Ralph looked from Anna to Harry, then back again.

"There are many strange things happening in and around Mystery Mansion . . . and not just nightmares that seem to come true," he said. "Those who seem to be enemies could well be friends but, far more frighteningly, friends could turn out to be foe."

A silence fell around the table, only to be interrupted by Harry's tummy gurgling. All three of them burst out laughing. Harry turned bright red.

"But why don't you want people to recognize you, Ralph?" continued Anna. "Forgive me for asking, but have you done something wrong?"

Ralph laughed. "Well, to start with, I must confess that my real name isn't Ralph," he said. "I have good reasons for not wanting certain people to know I'm in these parts. I'm up against the Jack O'Lantern, and –"

"Who is Jack O'Lantern?" Harry interrupted. "Is he behind all the strange happenings around Mystery Mansion?"

"It's not a man we're up against, Harry," said the man who called himself Ralph. "If only Jack O'Lantern was really flesh and blood. No. He's no human being. He's far more dangerous than that . . ."

29

What Next?

Ralph wouldn't answer any more questions there and then. "There's work to be done," he said. Harry and Anna couldn't go back to work at Mystery Mansion but, at the same time, they couldn't stay with Ralph forever, either. There was the added problem that the few things they did own between them were still back at the house.

"That's easily solved," said Ralph. "I have a friend inside the household. He can gather together your belongings and leave them somewhere nearby for you to collect."

"Who is he?" asked Harry excitedly.

"That must remain a secret. He will not be told that you are both alive, and I won't reveal his identity. It's only fair."

Ralph explained that he usually stayed indoors until after dark, except when he had to attend to "matters of some urgency". Obviously, today he had a number of these to attend to because he went out that afternoon. He didn't wrap bandages around his head, but he did wrap a large scarf across the lower half of his face and pulled a large hat down to his eyes. Harry thought he was unrecognizable.

Left alone in the cottage, Anna and Harry began to realize just how upside down their lives had been turned. To go from being a maid and a boot boy, to stumbling on some extraordinary events and now be thought dead.

Harry wished he could make sense of all he had seen. The trap door in the kitchen. The digging in the chapel ruins. The man who called himself Ralph, and the Jack O'Lantern that was not a person but a *thing*.

And there was something vaguely familiar about their handsome host who had saved him from the jaws of Lazarus, and them both from a slow and awful death in the marsh . . . and he *had* seen those terrifying skeletons. He knew it. They had been so real. Harry wanted to find out more.

30

They decided to search the cottage for clues, although they did feel rather guilty at taking advantage of their host's hospitality. What kind of clues they were looking for, they weren't sure. Something to reveal his identity perhaps.

Harry had just entered a small study when there was a knock at the window. He looked up, and his jaw dropped in amazement.

At the other side of the leaded pane glass stood Miss Charlotte Rakenhell, like he had never seen her before. There was a look of complete and utter amazement on her face.

She raised a dainty white-gloved hand and pointed to him through the glass.

"You're dead!" she cried. "You . . . you thief. You're supposed to be dead!"

News from Mystery Mansion

Harry dashed to the front door of the cottage and steered the stunned Charlotte inside. She sat herself in an armchair. He had so much to tell her . . . about her father ordering Mr. Paulfrey to dig in the ruins of the chapel at the dead of night . . . about the skeletons . . . about Ralph and this cottage.

Harry frowned. "How did you know where to find us?" he asked.

"You must be Anna," said Charlotte, ignoring the question. "I was told you were both dead, but here you are, with Harry looking healthier and happier than I've ever seen him before. Extraordinary."

"Who said I was dead?" asked Harry. "And what did you mean by calling me a thief just then?"

Charlotte leaned forward and told Harry and Anna what had happened the night before . . .

"But that's a lie!" cried Anna. "We didn't steal anything."

"I'm no thief," said Harry indignantly. "That story must have been made up to hide the true facts and to explain our disappearance."

"Then you must come back with me to Mystery Mansion right this minute. We must tell my father of Paulfrey's lies," said Charlotte, leaping to her feet.

Harry took a deep breath. "It's not that simple, miss," he said nervously. "Mr. Paulfrey may be spreading those lies on your father's instructions!"

A Doctor Named Grimm

While Harry and Anna were listening to Charlotte's story of Mr. Paulfrey's lies, Magnus Duggan lay in a windowless room less than a mile away. He had to rely on the woman nursing him to tell him the time of day.

He soon gathered that the woman only came to sit with him at night. Now that the headaches had lessened and his vision had improved, she had introduced herself as Mrs. Weatherspoon, housekeeper of Mystery Mansion. This puzzled the clock winder. Why should Lord Rakenhell's housekeeper be caring for him?

Apart from the one visit from the Lord of Mystery Mansion and one or two from Mr. Paulfrey, the only other person Duggan had met was standing by his bed now.

"Didn't I say that I would have our patient talking in no time? How are you feeling, Mr. Duggan?" he asked.

"Much better, thank you. Are you by any chance the doctor?" asked the clock winder.

"Indeed I am, Mr. Duggan. I apologize for not having formally introduced myself," said the man. "My name is Roylott Grimm."

"Dr. Roylott Grimm? Lord Rakenhell's personal doctor!" said the patient with surprise. "But what are you doing caring for me, just a humble clock winder with a bump on my head?"

"There's been a great deal more wrong with you than that my good man," said the doctor. "What about your nightmares? What about the vampire bats?"

34

In the flickering candle light, the doctor's eyes gleamed. Standing half in shadow, his cloak made him look strangely bat–like himself.

Magnus Duggan tried to sit up, but the effort was too great for him, and he rested his head back down on the pillow. "They were just dreams – nightmares – as you yourself said, sir."

Dr. Roylott Grimm rummaged around in his black bag. "Those who suffer nightmares on the estate of Mystery Mansion do not suffer *ordinary* nightmares, Mr. Duggan," he said. "More often than not, their nightmares eventually appear to come true."

Dr. Grimm produced a large syringe full of blue liquid and advanced toward the bed. "This is for your own good. Trust me," he smiled.

Duggan felt the prick in his arm, and immediately began to feel sleepy . . . sleepy . . . sleepy . . . His head began to spin and all he could focus on was Dr. Roylott Grimm's face – the words 'Jack O'Lantern', echoing inside his head.

Living Nightmares

Thora Mulch, the village gossip, had never been more than a few miles from the village in her entire life. She had been born in the village, been to school in the village and married in the village. She knew every building, every tree and every corner of every street. She knew everybody and everybody's business.

She was proud of her reputation as the local gossip. The old woman made a career of it, even more so since her husband had died a few years back. But until now, she hadn't actually *believed* much of what she said about the strange happenings at Mystery Mansion.

But now Thora had been having terrible nightmares. Nightmares that her dear departed husband, Norman had come back from the dead. He had died one night when he tripped over their cat, Jago, and broke his neck. The nightmare always began with the yowl of the cat and then Norman came toward her, his neck strangely twisted and his head lolling forward on his chest. It all seemed so real. Thora was very frightened.

Thora Mulch didn't tell anyone of the dream that haunted her night after night. She was beginning to be afraid to go out – except, of course, for her trips to *The Bogside Inn*. Hadn't Magnus Duggan's dreams of bats come true, and now he'd disappeared? What might happen to her?

Then Thora began to think back to other villagers in the past. Old Ma Gibbon who had thrown herself under a cart screaming that the witch hunters were after her. Thomas Bridmore who had disappeared from the village claiming that every night the shadows on his walls cried out to him. Thora shuddered and pulled her shawl tighter around her. Would she be next?

Outside, the wind was blowing, blanketing the village in mist. But Jago needed feeding so Thora had to go out. She sighed and stepped outside, setting off in the direction of the butcher. There was no one else around. Then she thought she heard footsteps – slow, deliberate footsteps somewhere behind her. But when she stopped, the footsteps stopped, so she started off again . . . as did the footsteps behind her. "Who's there?" she demanded, peering through the mist.

Thora could just make out a shadowy form with a strangely twisted neck and lolling head. She screamed, collapsing to the ground in a crumpled heap.

Full Circle

I can't believe what you're saying Harry.

Back at the cottage, Charlotte Rakenhell's mind was reeling. "Are you trying to tell me that my father is behind some . . . some dreadful plot?" she spluttered.

"I hate to be disrespectful," said Anna. "But it does seem likely. I mean, Mr. Paulfrey does work for his lordship –"

"But as I've said to Harry before, Paulfrey is such a horrid man," said Charlotte, throwing open the front door and stepping outside. "He could be up to no good right under my father's nose."

Pulling on their warm clothes, Harry and Anna caught up with Charlotte. They came to the edge of the wood, and there was the river in front of them, with a fallen tree stretching across it like a bridge, and a hollow oak tree off to the left. It was there that Harry had been supposed to leave the package for Mr. Colly.

"This is where I rescued you!" he cried. Charlotte nodded.

"Rescue? What rescue?" asked Anna, looking from Harry to Charlotte and back again.

"Never mind," said Charlotte.

"You still haven't told us how you found us, Miss Charlotte," said Harry, looking around him. He had been brought to the cottage when unconscious, and Anna had been led there in the dark. Neither of them knew where they were.

"It was quite by chance," confessed Charlotte. "I was so upset by the news that you'd been sucked up by the marsh that . . ." she paused and turned away. "I wanted to be alone. I'd no idea that the old woodcutter's cottage was being lived in. It's been empty for years. I passed it quite by chance, and there you both were sitting inside . . . alive and well."

"So you've no idea who the man who calls himself Ralph is, Miss Charlotte?" said Anna. "He's been very good to us. He saved our lives –"

"And gave us breakfast," Harry added.

Charlotte shook her head. "I doubt Father knows he's there either. I haven't heard any talk of a new tenant. Very strange. I wonder what this Ralph of yours is up to."

"Hey!" cried Harry. "I've just had a thought. Ralph said that he had a friend back at Mystery Mansion who could get us our belongings. That might be Mr. Colly, the head gardener. He gave me a package once and told me to put it in that tree over there." He pointed to the hollow oak. "Perhaps it was for Ralph, as his cottage is so close by."

"Why don't we ask him?" suggested Anna. "Here he comes now."

Sure enough, Ralph's figure had appeared, skirting the edge of the woodland. His hat was pulled low and his face was still covered by a scarf. What horrified the three children, however, was what he was carrying. It appeared to be the lifeless form of a woman.

A Face from the Past

Hurrying back to the cottage, Harry threw open the front door and stood aside to let Ralph past. Ralph gently laid the woman in an armchair. "You'll find some smelling salts in that cupboard, Harry," said Ralph. "Could you get them for me?"

"Who is she?" asked Anna.

Ralph moved the woman to a sitting position. "Her name is Thora Mulch," he said. "I gave her a fright when I came out of the mist. She seemed to think that I was someone named Norman."

On hearing the name, Thora Mulch opened an eye and moaned: "Norman? Is that you? Have you come back for me?"

Ralph wafted the smelling salts under her nose. "You're safe here, Mrs. Mulch. You're with friends."

When the smelling salts had worked their magic, Charlotte stepped forward from behind the chair. "I think that you owe us an explanation, sir," she said to Ralph. "And you could start by telling us your real name and what you are doing on my father's estate."

Ralph grinned and stood up. "I don't have to ask who *you* are," he chuckled. "I know I have the pleasure of addressing Miss Charlotte Lydia Rakenhell.

"Then you have me at an advantage, sir," said Charlotte.

Ralph roared with laughter, which seemed to upset Mrs. Mulch. He patted her hand and whispered soothing words.

"My identity can wait," he said. "Anna, please will you make Mrs. Mulch some tea. You'll find some in the kitchen."

Anna went out to the hand pump outside the back door to draw some water for the tea. She had just begun to lower the handle when she heard a loud growl. It was the deep, throaty snarl of Lazarus. The maid froze in fear.

"Oh, look who's here," said a cruel voice. "So little Anna isn't dead at all, but hiding out in the woods."

Anna turned to face Mr. Paulfrey, who was having trouble holding Lazarus on his leash. The steam from the dog's slavering jaws rose into the cold air like smoke from a dragon's mouth.

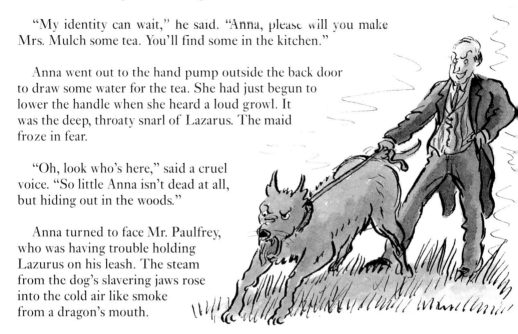

"I –I–I can explain . . ." Anna whimpered, terrified by the sight of the dog.

"Explain?" said Mr. Paulfrey. "What is there to explain? If everyone already thinks you're dead, then why disappoint them?" He bent down and unclasped Lazarus's collar from the leash. "Kill!" he screamed, a crazed laugh rising in his throat.

The Rage

Meanwhile, in the library at Mystery Mansion, Lord Rackenhell was in a rage. He hurled a glass across the room and it shattered into a thousand shards. "Are you telling me you don't know where my daughter is?" he bellowed.

Mrs. Weatherspoon, the victim of his lordship's rage, did not flinch. "Mr. Paulfrey is looking for Miss Charlotte now, your lordship," she reassured him. "There is no cause for alarm."

Rakenhell snorted like a wounded bull elephant. "*No cause for alarm*, you say? I have a son and heir who has deserted me. I have a house and estate built on this godforsaken marsh, and idiots like you and Paulfrey for servants . . . and you say that there is no cause for alarm. I want my daughter. *Now!*"

Mrs. Weatherspoon scowled and put her hands on her hips. "Your lordship – Henry – in the past you have asked me to tell you if and when you start behaving like a spoiled child. Well, I have to tell you. You are behaving like a spoiled child right now."

Lord Rakenhell went the brightest shade of purple the housekeeper had ever seen. "*What did you say?*" he screamed. "You should be taken from this place and horsewhipped woman."

Mrs. Weatherspoon continued to scowl. "If that isn't further proof that your lordship is behaving like a spoiled child, I don't know what is. If that will be all, I have other duties."

To her utter amazement, Rakenhell threw himself to the ground and began to pummel the polished wooden floor with his fists. "I am your lord and master!" he yelled. "My word is law!" Somehow, he became entangled in a tiger skin rug and appeared to be wrestling with a live creature. "Get this thing off me!" he howled. "Get it off."

At that moment, Dr. Roylott Grimm entered the library. He had heard the commotion from the hallway and was already brandishing a syringe when he entered the room. "Calm yourself, Henry! Calm yourself!" he urged.

Mrs. Weatherspoon sat on Lord Rakenhell to keep him still while Dr. Grimm administered the injection into his arm. The tiger skin lay lifeless on the floor. "We're going to have to get his lordship and Miss Charlotte away from here," said the housekeeper. "He can't take much more of this."

"None of us can, Mrs. Weatherspoon," said the doctor, feeling the pulse of Lord Rakenhell who was now drifting off into sleep. "Jack O'Lantern is working his evil into all of us. He could ruin us all yet. He could ruin us all."

The Master

A split second before Lazarus launched himself on top of the terrified Anna, a voice rang out through the woods like a gun shot. "No boy!" cried Ralph, and the hound slumped to the ground with ears flat, whimpering like a harmless puppy.

It was hard to tell who was more stunned, Anna or Mr. Paulfrey. Both of them were shaking – Mr. Paulfrey with anger and Anna with fear, which was now turning to relief. Harry and Charlotte tumbled out of the back door to see what all the commotion was about.

"Paulfrey, what are you doing here?" demanded the young Miss Rakenhell.

"Looking for you Miss," explained the butler. "It seems I've uncovered a whole hornets' nest. I don't think your father will be too pleased to hear that you have been mixing with thieving servants . . . and whoever this may be." His gaze locked on to Ralph's face. "I feel sure *we*'ve met before," he said.

"Of course we have, Paulfrey," sneered Ralph, with a coldness in his voice the children had not heard before. "I wouldn't expect Charlotte to remember me too clearly. She was so young when I went away. But you, Paulfrey? Look at this face. Older, perhaps, but have I really changed that much?"

The butler's jaw dropped. "It's . . . you're . . ."

Ralph whistled through his teeth and Lazarus bounded over to him. "Yes Paulfrey. I'm Edmund Rakenhell, who you were so cruel to as a boy. My father was too busy battling Jack O'Lantern to listen to me. Perhaps he'll listen now."

It was Charlotte's turn to be stunned. Ralph was none other than her long lost brother, heir to Mystery Mansion and nothing but a dim memory until now. "Edmund!" she whooped with delight, throwing herself at him.

"Welcome back, Master Edmund," said Mr. Paulfrey, with a sneer. "I'm afraid you'll find your poor father still the same as ever . . . only more so. Quite off his head in fact." He laughed.

"Tell me something I don't already know, Paulfrey. I'm here to put a stop to all this madness. My father's madness, his rages and all the unspeakable nightmares that have gripped the villagers for far too long," said Edmund.

"I somehow doubt that," said Mr. Paulfrey.

"My father, Dr. Grimm, Mrs. Weatherspoon and all the others have been trying to do some good but what they didn't realize was that *you* have been turning everything to your own advantage," said Edmund. "You don't want my father to be cured or clear-headed. You want Jack O'Lantern to get him like the rest of them. But you've failed, Paulfrey. You've failed."

"Don't think you've beaten me yet – any of you!" Paulfrey cried. He turned and ran, leaving a trail of terrifying laughter behind him. It was the laughter of a madman.

45

Back at Mystery Mansion

Harry and Anna returned to Mystery Mansion in style. They went through the main entrance and into the drawing room with Edmund and Charlotte. Here, Lord Rakenhell was resting on a couch, flanked by Mrs. Weatherspoon and Dr. Roylott Grimm. Mrs. Weatherspoon recognized Edmund Rakenhell at once, and there was much weeping and hugging all around.

When the excitement of reunion was over, attention turned to Harry and Anna who looked out of place in all this grandeur. "And who are these two?" asked Lord Rakenhell, quietly.

"The two servants you thought had perished in the marshland when chased by Lazarus, father," said Edmund.

"The thieves!" said his lordship, struggling to sit up. "But at least you're alive. No one deserves to die in that marsh."

"Not thieves, but innocent children who stumbled on your secrets beneath the kitchen and your digging by the ruined chapel, father. I've no doubt Paulfrey took advantage of the situation and stole some of the silver for himself. He's been cheating you for years," said Edmund. "We owe Harry and Anna here an explanation."

Lord Rakenhell sighed. "And I trusted him. I am at the end of my tether. After generations, I think that the Rakenhells should admit defeat and leave Mystery Mansion. Let nature and Jack O'Lantern reclaim this terrible part of the country."

"I don't understand," protested Anna. "How can this Jack O'Lantern have the Rakenhells on the run?"

"Jack O'Lantern is just one of its names. Another is will-o'-the-wisp or *ignis fatuus*," explained Dr. Grimm. "It's the pale glow you sometimes see over the marshland around Mystery Mansion at night. It's caused by the mixture of gases created by decomposing organic matter — "

Harry and Anna looked at him blankly. "What the doctor means, is that the rotting plants in the marshland mix together to form strange marsh gases," said Edmund Rakenhell. "It's these gases which gave this house the name *Misty Mansion*. And that give people nightmares and make them see things."

"You have to breathe a lot of the marsh gas over many years for it to affect the mind badly," the doctor reassured them. "Mr. Duggan, who we are caring for in the hideaway under the kitchen, has lived in the village for fifty years and it has only recently started to muddle his brain and make him see imaginary bats. Not one of us in this room has been seriously affected . . . except his lordship –"

"Who has made it his life to try to find a way to beat the marsh gas, without letting on to outsiders that it is anything more than a bad-smelling mist," Edmund Rakenhell interrupted. "Hence hiding away and caring for the sick, and taking soil samples from the chapel. Sadly, Jack O'Lantern has given you rages, father, and let Paulfrey trick you at every turn."

"But what made you come back?" Harry asked.

"I haven't wasted my years away from Mystery Mansion. I've come back to stay. We all can. I'm a man of science and have spent my time researching the problem," said Edmund proudly. "By growing certain new plants in the marshland, we'll be able to produce a new gas – one which makes all the other gases harmless. The nightmares will be over for everyone. Once and for all."

Did You Spot?

You can use this page to help spot things that could be useful in solving the mystery. First, there are hints and clues you can read as you go along. They will give you some idea of what to look out for. Then there are extra notes to read which tell you more about what happened afterwards.

Hints and Clues

3	The grave digger's nightmare appears to have come true.
4-5	The parcel could be an important clue to someone's identity later.
8-9	What could have happened to the package?
10-11	Hmm. Another example of nightmares coming to life?
12-13	There can be more than just a supernatural explanation for the blank wall.
14-15	Plenty of big, old houses have cellars.
16-17	Mystery, Misty, Misery or Miserly. What's in a name?
18-19	The soil itself might be important.
22-23	Lazarus was quick to obey the bandaged stranger. Could he know him?
24-25	Is that a *square* of light in the roof above Duggan? Where could he be being held?
26-27	Surely it's a little strange to have a picture of a plant in a photo frame?
28-29	Lanterns give off light.
30-31	Study the items in the room with care.
34-35	Ah. So could it be that Magnus Duggan is being kept in the cellar?
36-37	The figure in the mist looks familiar.
38-39	You should know who Ralph is carrying.
40-41	How could Ralph know Charlotte?
42-43	From the way Mrs. Weatherspoon has been talking, his lordship sounds ill.
44-45	Everything should begin to fall into place from now on.

In the End

Edmund Rakenhell's plan to make the marsh gases around Mystery Mansion harmless worked. Today, there are still mists in the village and near the house, but they neither glow in the dark, nor make people see things.

Magnus Duggan and Thora Mulch both made full recoveries.

Life at Mystery Mansion changed for everyone after Edmund's return. On Dr. Grimm's orders, Lord Rakenhell went to Europe to get better. Edmund took over the running of the house and the servants became some of the best-treated for miles around.

When Harry grew up, he became a butler. Miss Charlotte married a man called Lord Snortle and had seven children.

Inspired by Edmund's example, Anna became fascinated by plants. With help from the Rakenhell family, she was awarded a university scholarship. She later became one of the world's leading experts on plant life.

The body of Mr. Paulfrey was found floating in the marshland near Mystery Mansion. Jack O'Lantern had claimed one last victim.

By the way . . .

The doorway behind the tapestry (on page 13) was bricked up by Mr. Paulfrey. He had filled the storage cupboard with his ill-gotten gains. Over the years, he stole a great deal from the house.

Did you spot the items in the room on page 31? – a microscope on the table to help Edmund with his experiments and a picture on the wall of him as a child with Lord Rakenhell.

First published in 1995 by Usborne Publishing Ltd, Usborne House, 83-85 Saffron Hill, London EC1N 8RT, England. Copyright © 1995 Usborne Publishing Ltd.

The name Usborne and the device 🎈 are Trade Marks of Usborne Publishing Ltd.

Printed in Great Britain U.E.

First published in America March 1996